Everyone Reads

written by Pam Holden
illustrated by Deborah C. Johnson

My mother likes to cook.
She makes good food. Yum!

She reads books about cooking.

My father likes to play sports.
He likes to watch games, too.

He reads books about sports.

My big brother likes planes.
He makes model planes.

He reads books about planes.

My sister likes to dance.
She has a dancing dress.

She reads books about dancing.

My grandfather likes fishing.
He likes to catch fish.

10

He reads books about fishing.

My grandmother likes flowers.
She has flowers in her garden.

She reads books about gardens.

My little brother likes animals.
He likes going to the zoo.

He looks at books about animals.

I like to read books about rockets!